KATY DIDN'T

Written by Johnny Cuomo
Illustrated by Benjamin Lowery

Peter Pauper Press, Inc.
WHITE PLAINS, NEW YORK

Published by Peter Pauper Press, Inc.
202 Mamaroneck Avenue
White Plains, New York 10601 USA

Library of Congress Cataloging-in-Publication Data

Names: Cuomo, Johnny, author. | Lowery, Benjamin, 1984- illustrator.
Title: Katy didn't / written by Johnny Cuomo ; illustrated by Benjamin Lowery.
Other titles: Katy did not
Description: First edition. | White Plains, New York : Peter Pauper Press, Inc., 2020. | Audience: Grades K-1.
Summary: Being the new bug at school can be tough, because the other bugs are sometimes not very
welcoming--except for Katydid who is kind and caring, and so a new friendship is formed.
Identifiers: LCCN 2020011515 | ISBN 9781441334534 (hardcover)
Subjects: LCSH: Katydids--Juvenile fiction. | Insects--Juvenile fiction. |
First day of school--Juvenile fiction. | Friendship--Juvenile fiction. |
CYAC: Katydids--Fiction. | Insects--Fiction. | First day of school--Fiction. | Friendship--Fiction.
Classification: LCC PZ7.1.C6764 Kat 2020 | DDC [E]--dc23
LC record available at https://lccn.loc.gov/2020011515

ISBN 978-1-4413-3453-4

Manufactured for Peter Pauper Press, Inc.
Printed in Hong Kong

7 6 5 4 3 2 1

Visit us at www.peterpauper.com

For all the "new bugs" of the world.

Thanks to Kristin, Johnny, Paul, Mom, Dad, Lisa, students, and teachers—past and present,
Ben, Dan, and E.B.G. who taught me to "Never Give Up."
J.C.

To my nieces and nephews, Alei'a, Peter, Gianna, Benedict, and Delia
B.L.

A new bug came to school today.

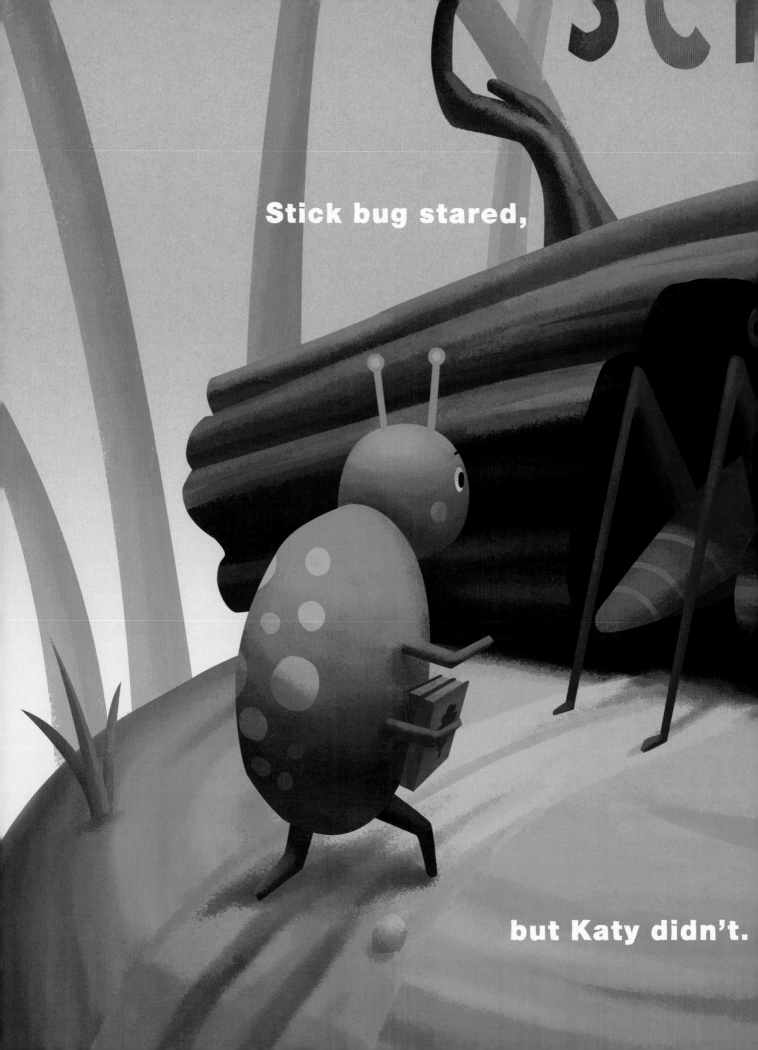

Stick bug stared,

but Katy didn't.

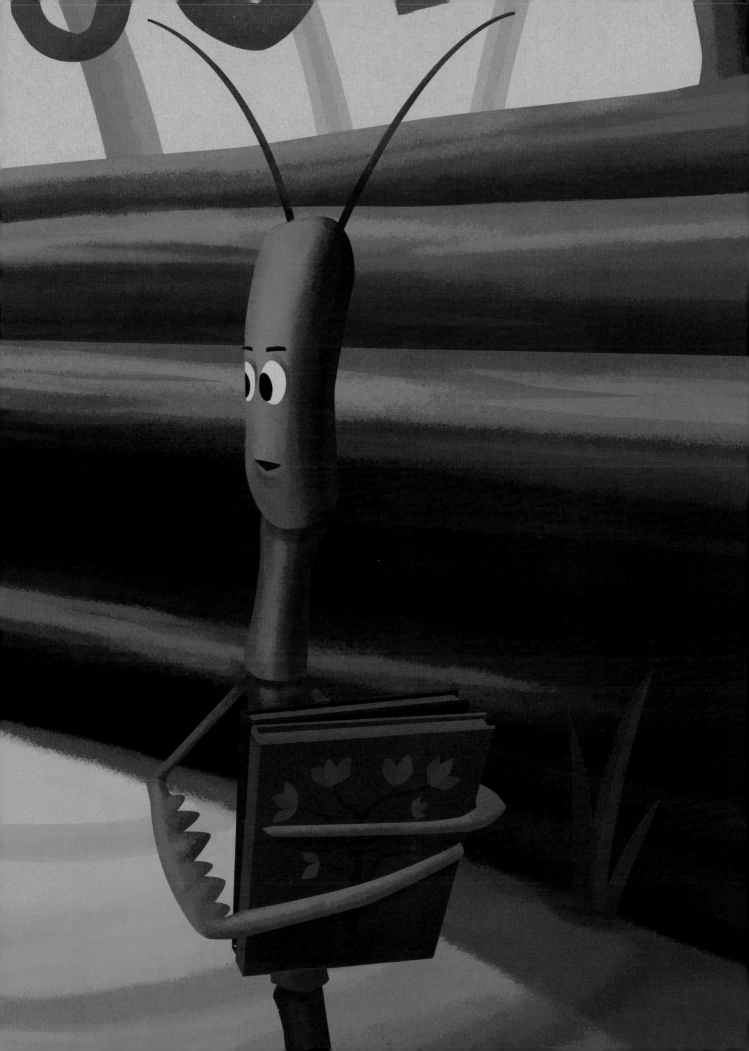

Pill bug made faces,

but Katy didn't.

Potato bug
whispered secrets,

but Katy didn't.

Lightning bug laughed,

but Katy didn't.

Ladybug moved away,

but Katy didn't.

At the end of the day,
the teacher asked the new bug...

Katydid!

Katydid!

And she did.